# Echoes of Star Haven

By Kristine Hawkins

*Inspired by the Poetry of Harriett Atherton Croskrey*

*In memory of her mother, whose legacy lives on in words, love, and the laughter of her grandsons.*

*This book is a testament to the enduring strength of family bonds, the healing power of art, and the timeless connection between past and present. May the echoes of love, resilience, and hope continue to inspire all who turn these pages.*

***Author's Note***

Writing *Echoes of Star Haven* has been a deeply personal journey for me, one that intertwines my own family's history with the fictional world of Clara, Mia, and Sophie. This story is inspired by my mother's poetry and the life she led. My mother, Harriett Croskrey, lost her own mother in a tragic car accident when she was just twelve years old. This devastating event led her to grow up in an orphanage and foster homes, shaping her resilience and strength in ways I can only imagine. Her poetry has always been a source of inspiration for me, a testament to her enduring spirit and the power of words to heal and connect.

My name is Kristine Hawkins, and I was born and raised in the San Francisco Bay Area of California. I am blessed with a loving husband, three wonderful sons, and two amazing stepchildren. By profession, I am a nurse, a role that has taught me the importance of compassion, empathy, and the strength of the human spirit. Balancing my career with my passion for writing has been a rewarding challenge, and I am grateful for the support of my family in pursuing my dreams.

*Echoes of Star Haven* is a tribute to my mother's legacy and to all those who have faced adversity with courage and grace. It is a story about love, resilience, and the enduring connections that bind us together, even across time and space. I hope that readers find solace, inspiration, and a sense of belonging.

Thank you for joining me on this journey.

With heartfelt gratitude,

Kristine Hawkins

**Rich and Emotional Storytelling**: The narrative beautifully captures the struggles and triumphs of Clara, from her stormy beginnings to her eventual reconciliation with her daughters. The emotional depth is evident in the detailed descriptions and the heartfelt dialogues

**Complex and Relatable Characters**: Each character is well-developed, with their own unique struggles and growth. Clara's journey from a lonely child in an orphanage to a determined mother seeking justice and connection is inspiring. Mia and Sophie's evolution from feeling distant from their mother to understanding and supporting her adds a touching layer to the story.

**Thematic Depth**: The book explores deep themes like single motherhood, the search for identity, the impact of the past on the present, and the healing power of creativity. These themes are handled with sensitivity and nuance, making the story resonate with readers on a personal level.

**Integration of Poetry**: Clara's poetry adds a lyrical and reflective dimension to the story. It provides insight into her innermost thoughts and emotions, enriching the narrative. The idea of including a poetry collection at the end ties the book together nicely, offering readers a deeper connection to Clara's experiences.

**Mystery and Discovery**: The elements of mystery, such as the hidden room, the secret documents, and the journey to uncover Evelyn's past, keep the reader engaged. These plot points add suspense and drive the story forward, making it hard to put the book down.

**Uplifting Conclusion**: The story's conclusion, with Clara finding peace, reconnecting with her daughters, and discovering the legacy of Star Haven, is uplifting and satisfying. It leaves readers with a sense of hope and the enduring power of family and love.

## Table of Contents

- Selected Poems
- Reflections on Love and Resilience
- Poems Dedicated to Mia and Sophie

## Chapter 1: Clara's Early Life

### Stormy Beginnings

Clara's story began on a tempestuous night in the small coastal town of Havenbrook. The wind howled like a chorus of restless spirits, and the rain lashed against the old, creaky house where she was born, each droplet racing down the windows as if trying to escape the storm's fury. Inside, Evelyn, Clara's mother, endured the trials of childbirth alone, save for the presence of a seasoned midwife. The storm outside mirrored Evelyn's inner turbulence—a maelstrom of pain, determination, and the raw, primal strength required to bring her daughter into the world.

Evelyn, a struggling artist with a soul deeply attuned to the sea, channeled her surroundings into her art. Her paintings often depicted the storm-tossed waves crashing against rugged cliffs, capturing the raw, untamed beauty of nature. On the night Clara was born, the sea's fury seemed to synchronize with Evelyn's labor, each crash of thunder resonating with her cries, and each flash of lightning illuminating the room like a fleeting beacon of hope.

Despite her fierce spirit, Evelyn's strength waned rapidly after Clara's birth. The toll of a hard life and the intense strain of childbirth left her fragile and weakened. Cradling her newborn daughter with hands that trembled from exhaustion, Evelyn whispered a few words of love and hope, her voice barely audible over the storm's roar. As the first light of dawn began to creep through the storm clouds, Evelyn's life slipped away. Before she passed, knowing the scandal that surrounded her and wanting to protect Clara, she entrusted her newborn daughter to Mrs. Teal, the midwife who assisted her, ensuring Clara would be hidden from the dangers she feared.

**Life in the Orphanage**

Clara was taken in by the local orphanage, a large, somber edifice that loomed on the edge of town like a sentinel of lost childhoods. The orphanage was a place of stark contrasts—its imposing stone walls and iron gates stood in sharp contrast to the warmth of a family home. The matrons and staff, while stern, provided the necessities of life: food, clothing, and education.

Yet, the emotional warmth and sense of belonging that Clara needed were conspicuously absent.

The orphanage's dormitories were filled with the sounds of children's laughter and occasional tears, but the connections Clara formed with her fellow orphans were fleeting. Many were adopted and left, their departures leaving gaps that were rarely filled by newcomers. The transient nature of these friendships left Clara with a deep sense of solitude.

From a young age, Clara found solace in a battered, worn-out notebook her mother had left behind. The pages were filled with Evelyn's delicate sketches, half-finished paintings, and fragments of poetry, each one a whisper of the mother Clara never had a chance to know. Clara would lose herself in these pages for hours, tracing the lines of her mother's art and feeling an ethereal connection to the woman who had given her life. Inspired by Evelyn's unfinished works, Clara began to write her own poems, her words becoming a conduit for the complex emotions she struggled to understand.

Mrs. Teal, the orphanage's matron, was a woman of formidable presence. Her strict demeanor was tempered by a hidden warmth that emerged in her interactions with Clara. Recognizing the spark of talent in the young girl, Mrs. Teal encouraged Clara's passion for writing. She often found Clara tucked away in a quiet nook of the orphanage, absorbed in a book or scribbling furiously in her notebook. Despite her stern exterior, Mrs. Teal had a soft spot for Clara, often providing her with extra paper and pens—small but significant gestures that supported Clara's budding creativity

## Chapter 2: Moving to Sunnyvale

### *A New Beginning*

As Clara reached the cusp of adulthood, the yearning to escape the confines of the orphanage grew stronger. When she turned eighteen, she gathered her scant belongings—most notably, her mother's cherished notebook—and stepped into the unknown. The dusty roads of her old life gave way to the promise of new beginnings as she journeyed to Sunnyvale, a town that seemed straight out of a storybook.

Sunnyvale was a charming, picturesque haven with cobblestone streets that meandered past quaint cottages adorned with flowering window boxes. The town's vibrant arts community was palpable in the air, and Clara felt an almost magnetic pull toward it. She was drawn to the way the town’s rich history seemed to seep into every brick and every whisper of the wind.

Upon her arrival, Clara found employment at a local café, a cozy establishment with an eclectic mix of mismatched furniture and walls lined with shelves crammed with books. The café, with its warm, inviting ambiance and the rich aroma of freshly brewed coffee, quickly became a sanctuary for Clara. Maria, the café’s owner, was a kind-hearted woman with an artistic past of her own. She had an intuitive understanding of Clara’s needs and offered her not only a job but also a small, charming apartment above the café. The apartment, with its gabled roof and skylight, became Clara's new sanctuary.

### *Falling in Love*

Settling into her new life in Sunnyvale, Clara found joy in the café's comforting routines. The clink of coffee cups, the murmur of conversations, and the occasional burst of laughter from patrons provided a rhythmic soundtrack to her days. She reveled in the simple pleasure of serving coffee and chatting with customers.

One of the café's regulars was a man named Daniel, who made the corner booth his own personal refuge. With his dark, curly hair and intense blue eyes that seemed to pierce through the veneer of everyday life, Daniel was a writer whose presence commanded attention. He was often found typing away on his laptop, lost in the world of his own creation.

Daniel was a quiet, introspective soul whose passion for literature matched Clara's own. His conversations were thoughtful and deep, and as they began to share their favorite books and delve into their own writing projects, a profound connection blossomed. Clara found herself captivated by Daniel's insights and the way he seemed to understand her unspoken thoughts.

Their friendship gradually evolved into romance, and Clara experienced a profound joy she had never known before. Daniel's presence filled the void in her heart, and the moments they spent together became precious treasures. They would often take leisurely walks along the beach, hand in hand, as the waves caressed their feet. The sea, which had once symbolized Clara's loneliness, now mirrored the depth of her newfound love.

Their walks were filled with shared dreams and whispered secrets, and Clara marveled at the way Daniel's laughter seemed to blend with the rhythm of the ocean. The sea, a constant companion in Clara's life, now appeared to reflect the warmth and promise of her relationship with Daniel.

However, the joy they shared was fleeting. When Clara discovered she was pregnant, the news struck Daniel with a force that left him reeling. His initial shock gave way to fear, and he struggled with the reality of impending fatherhood. The weight of responsibility overwhelmed him, and he began to distance himself from Clara. The once warm and comforting relationship became strained, and eventually, Daniel made the heart-wrenching decision to leave town, leaving Clara alone once more, her heart heavy with loss and uncertainty.

## Chapter 3: Raising Mia and Sophie

### *The Struggles of Single Motherhood*

Clara's determination to provide a loving home for her twin daughters, Mia and Sophie, burned brightly despite the many challenges she faced. The girls were born on a clear spring morning, their cries piercing through the small apartment above the café, a stark contrast to the serene weather outside. Clara cradled them close, feeling a profound surge of love and protectiveness that was both exhilarating and overwhelming. In their tiny, perfect faces, she saw the promise of a future filled with the stability and affection she had longed for in her own childhood.

Raising twins as a single mother was an immense undertaking. Clara juggled her responsibilities at the café with the demands of motherhood, her days filled with the cacophony of toddler laughter and the chaos of managing a household. Her nights were often consumed by work, staying up late after the girls had gone to bed to catch up on bills and prepare for the next day. Maria, ever the empathetic and perceptive friend, extended her support by offering Clara flexible work hours and extra assistance, becoming a surrogate grandmother to Mia and Sophie. Her warm presence provided a much-needed reprieve and a semblance of familial stability.

Despite Clara's tireless efforts, the weight of her responsibilities bore heavily on her. Her exhaustion was palpable, her mind frequently preoccupied with the endless cycle of work, bills, and the constant struggle to provide for her daughters. When she tried to assist Mia and Sophie with their homework, her divided attention often led to frustration. The vibrant, joyful atmosphere of their home gradually shifted to one of tension and misunderstanding, the playful banter replaced by strained silences.

### *Growing Distance*

Despite her best efforts, Clara felt like she was failing her daughters. The guilt and frustration gnawed at her, making it even harder to connect with them. She longed to be the mother she had always wished for, but the reality of her situation seemed insurmountable.

In her darkest moments, Clara turned to her poetry, pouring her heartache into her verses. She wrote:

### *The Distance Grows*

*In the mirror, I see her face,*

*A mother lost, a fall from grace.*

*Her children cry, she cannot hear,*

*Her heart is filled with doubt and fear.*

Clara knew she needed help, but the path to healing seemed daunting. She felt trapped in a cycle of guilt and inadequacy, unable to break free. The distance between her and her daughters grew wider, and she feared that she would never be able to bridge the gap.

### *A Difficult Decision*

The decision to let her daughters live with their father was the hardest Clara ever made. The days leading up to it were filled with sleepless nights and endless worry. Clara had always prided herself on being strong and independent, but the weight of single motherhood was becoming unbearable. The financial strain, the constant juggling of work and childcare, and the emotional toll were taking a heavy toll on her.

Clara's apartment, once filled with laughter and warmth, now felt like a battleground. Mia and Sophie, sensing their mother's stress, began to act out. Their once joyful home became a place of tension and tears. Clara found herself snapping at them over small things, her patience worn thin by exhaustion and anxiety.

One evening, after a particularly difficult day, Clara sat at the kitchen table, her head in her hands. The bills were piling up, and she had just received a notice from the landlord about a rent increase. The weight of her responsibilities felt like a crushing burden. She glanced at a photo of Mia and Sophie on the fridge, their smiling faces a stark contrast to the turmoil she felt inside.

Desperate for a solution, Clara reached out to Daniel, her daughters' father. They had remained on amicable terms, and he had always expressed a willingness to help. When she explained her situation, Daniel listened with empathy and concern. "Clara," he said gently, "maybe the girls should come stay with me for a while. It would give you a chance to get back on your feet."

The suggestion hit Clara like a punch to the gut. The thought of being separated from her daughters was unbearable, but deep down, she knew it might be the best option. She spent the next few days agonizing over the decision, her heart torn between her love for her daughters and the harsh reality of their situation.

Clara sought advice from Maria, the elderly woman who owned the bookstore café. Maria had become a trusted confidante, offering wisdom and support. “Sometimes,” Maria said softly, “we must make sacrifices for the ones we love. It doesn’t mean you love them any less. It means you’re doing what’s best for them.”

With a heavy heart, Clara made the decision. She sat Mia and Sophie down and explained the situation as gently as she could. “I love you both more than anything in this world,” she said, her voice trembling. “But right now, I need to make sure we have a stable home. You’ll be staying with your father for a while.”

The girls’ reactions were a mix of confusion and sadness. “But why, Mom?” Sophie asked, her eyes filling with tears. “We want to stay with you.”

Clara hugged them tightly, her own tears falling freely. “I know, sweetheart. And I want you here with me. But this is just for a little while. I promise we’ll be together again soon.”

As she packed their bags, Clara’s heart broke with every item she placed inside. She kissed their foreheads, whispering words of love and reassurance. Watching them drive away with Daniel, she felt a piece of her heart break. The guilt and fear of having made an irreparable mistake consumed her.

The days that followed were a blur of pain and loneliness. Clara found herself wandering through their empty rooms, clutching their favorite toys and clothes. She missed their laughter, their hugs, and the way they filled the house with life. The silence was deafening, and the emptiness was a constant reminder of her decision.

***A Mother's Sacrifice***

*In the quiet of the night, I hear their cries,*

*A mother's love, a fragile guise.*

*I reach out, but they slip away,*

*In my heart, they forever stay.*

## ***Chapter 4: A Fresh Start***

### ***Finding Hope in Seabrook***

Clara moved to the quaint town of Seabrook, a place she had always dreamed of visiting. As a child, she had written the name "Seabrook" many times, as it was where her mother was from. Clara hoped it would offer her the fresh start she so desperately needed.

Nestled along the rugged coastline, Seabrook was picturesque, with tree-lined streets, charming shops, and a close-knit community. The town's most iconic feature was its historic lighthouse, standing tall on a rocky promontory. The lighthouse, with its whitewashed walls and red roof, had guided ships safely to shore for generations. Its steady beam of light was a comforting presence, visible from nearly every part of the town.

Clara found a small apartment above a bookstore, its cozy interior filled with the scent of old books and freshly brewed coffee from the café downstairs. The apartment had a quaint charm, with sloping ceilings and a window that offered a perfect view of the lighthouse. Each evening, Clara would watch as the beam of light swept across the dark waters, a symbol of hope and guidance.

She threw herself into her work, taking a job at the local library. The library, a grand old building with high ceilings and stained-glass windows, stood near the town square. The quiet, orderly environment provided a stark contrast to the chaos she felt inside. Every day, she helped patrons find books, organized shelves, and planned community events, but her mind was never far from Mia and Sophie.

Nights were the hardest. Alone in her apartment, Clara would sit by the window, staring out at the twinkling lights of the town and the distant glow of the lighthouse. The silence was deafening, and the emptiness of the rooms echoed her own sense of loss. She often found herself reaching for her phone, longing to hear her daughters' voices, but fear and guilt held her back.

The lighthouse became a beacon of solace for Clara. She would often take late-night walks to the shore, where she could hear the waves crashing against the rocks and feel the cool sea breeze on her face. Standing near the lighthouse, she felt a connection to something larger than herself, a sense of stability and direction that she desperately needed. The rhythmic sound of the foghorn, mingling with the distant cries of seabirds, provided a strange comfort, a reminder that she was not alone in her struggles.

In the library, Clara found a way to channel her emotions into something positive. She started a poetry workshop, hoping to share her love of words and rhythm with others. The workshop quickly became popular, attracting a diverse group of people, from curious teenagers to elderly residents seeking a creative outlet. The joy and expression that filled the room during these sessions brought a spark of light to her otherwise lonely days. Slowly, she began to feel a part of the Seabrook community, finding friendship and support among her colleagues and the townspeople.

Sometimes, in the quiet hours at the library, Clara would sift through old records and local history books, hoping to find information about her mother. The mystery of her past and her mother's connection to Seabrook lingered in the back of her mind, fueling her desire to uncover her family's history. Each piece of information she found, no matter how small, was a treasure, bringing her a step closer to understanding her mother's life and the reasons she had cherished Seabrook.

### *Poetry as a Lifeline*

Inspired by the emotions flooding through her, Clara penned another poem, capturing the depth of her sorrow and the flicker of hope that refused to die:

Beneath the weight of night, my heart does break,
A sea of tears, an endless ache.
Yet in the dark, a light persists,
A beacon of hope, in the fog and mist.

Though distance keeps my loves away,
I dream we'll reunite someday.
The waves may crash, the winds may moan,
But in my heart, they've found a home.

Determined to reconnect with Mia and Sophie, Clara began writing letters to them. Each letter was a heartfelt attempt to bridge the gap that had grown between them. She poured her soul into every word, hoping to convey her love and regret.

***Letters to Mia and Sophie***

**Letter 1:**

My dearest Mia and Sophie,

I hope this letter finds you well. I miss you both more than words can express. Not a day goes by that I don't think of you and wish I could be there with you. I know I made mistakes, and I am so sorry for the pain I caused. Please know that I love you with all my heart.

I remember the times we spent together, the laughter and the joy. Those memories are my most treasured possessions. I hope that one day we can create new memories together. Until then, please know that I am always thinking of you and loving you from afar.

With all my love,
Mom

**Letter 2:**

My sweet girls,

I wanted to share a poem I wrote for you. It reflects my feelings and my hopes for our future.

*In the quiet of the night, I hear your laughter,*
*A distant echo, a haunting after.*
*Your faces in my dreams, so near,*
*Yet in the waking world, you disappear.*

*But in my heart, you always stay,*
*Guiding me through each passing day.*
*I long for the time we can be together,*
*To hold you close, now and forever.*

I love you both so much. Please write back if you can. I would love to hear from you.

With all my love,
Mom

**Letter 3:**

Dear Mia and Sophie,

I hope you are doing well in school and enjoying your time with your friends. I wanted to tell you about my new life here in Seabrook. It's a beautiful town, and I think you would love it. There's a lovely beach where I often go to think of you.

I know things have been difficult, and I understand if you are angry with me. I just want you to know that I am here, waiting for the day we can be together again. I am working on myself, trying to be the best mom I can be for you.

Please take care of each other and know that I am always here for you.

With all my love,
Mom

Clara's poetry became more than an outlet; it was her lifeline. Each verse was a testament to her pain and her resilience, a way to navigate the stormy seas of her emotions. As she continued to write and teach, she found that the lighthouse's unwavering light mirrored her own journey. Just as it guided ships through turbulent waters, her words guided her through the tumult of her heartache, leading her toward a place of peace and the promise of a brighter future.

## Chapter 5: Reconnecting with Her Daughters

### *A Long-Awaited Response*

Clara poured her heart into each letter she sent, her pen moving slowly as she carefully chose her words. Each envelope was a vessel of her deepest emotions, sealed with a hope that seemed both fragile and unwavering. She awaited a response with a mixture of trepidation and anticipation, checking the mailbox daily, her heart sinking with every empty visit.

The silence that followed was excruciating, a constant reminder of the distance that had grown between them. Yet, Clara clung to the belief that one day her daughters would grasp the depth of her love and understand her reasons for the separation. She envisioned their reunion, a day when the silence would be replaced by the warmth of their voices and the closeness of their embrace.

Then, one crisp morning, Clara's routine changed. As she reached into the mailbox, her fingers brushed against a familiar, comforting texture—the smooth surface of an envelope adorned with Mia's neat handwriting. Her heart skipped a beat, and her breath caught in her throat as she took the letter inside. With trembling fingers, she tore open the envelope and unfolded the letter within, her eyes scanning the heartfelt words:

Dear Mom,

Thank you for your letters. Sophie and I miss you a lot. It's been hard without you, but we're doing okay. We understand that you needed to take some time to get things sorted out. We hope you're doing better now.

We loved the poem you sent us. It made us feel closer to you. We want to see you again and spend time together. Maybe we can visit you in Seabrook?

Love, Mia and Sophie

Clara's eyes welled up with tears as she read the letter, each sentence a balm to her aching heart. It was the first tangible sign of healing, a glimmer of hope for a future reunion. Overwhelmed with joy and relief, she immediately penned a response, her words brimming with gratitude and eagerness. She proposed that they arrange a visit during the school break, envisioning the moment when their fractured family could begin to mend.

*A Joyful Reunion*

The day of Mia and Sophie's arrival was filled with a palpable sense of excitement. Clara stood at the bustling train station, her heart racing with anticipation. The crisp, salty air of Seabrook mingled with her nerves, and she scanned the crowd for familiar faces. When she finally spotted Mia and Sophie stepping off the train, their silhouettes becoming clearer with each passing second, Clara felt a surge of emotions that left her breathless.

As soon as they were within reach, Clara rushed forward, her arms opening wide. The embrace was tight and enveloping, a physical manifestation of the love and longing she had harbored for so long. "I've missed you both so much," she whispered, her voice breaking as tears streamed down her cheeks.

Sophie, her eyes shimmering with emotion, clung to her mother. "We missed you too, Mom," she said, her voice choked with the weight of their shared feelings. "We're so happy to see you."

Their visit was a journey through the life Clara had built in Seabrook. Clara guided them through the town's charming streets, where colorful blooms cascaded from window boxes and the scent of freshly baked pastries wafted through the air. They spent serene afternoons at the beach, where the waves lapped gently at their feet, and explored the bookstore café—a haven where Clara often found inspiration for her poetry.

Margaret, the café owner, greeted them with open arms and a warm smile. She served them fragrant tea and delicate pastries, her hospitality adding a touch of homeliness to their visit. The café, with its cozy nooks and eclectic décor, seemed to radiate the love and care Margaret had always extended to Clara and her family.

One evening, as they gathered around the crackling fireplace in Clara's modest apartment, the warmth of the flames mirrored the warmth Clara felt in her heart. Clara took a deep breath, her voice quivering as she began to share her story. "I want you to know that I never stopped loving you," she said, her eyes glistening with unshed tears. "I made mistakes, and I'm so sorry for the pain I caused. But I needed to find a way to be the best mother I could be for you."

Mia and Sophie listened with rapt attention, their expressions a blend of understanding and compassion. "We know, Mom," Mia said softly, her voice steady despite the emotions swirling within. “We were hurt and confused, but we understand now. We’re just glad to be with you again.”

The evening was filled with laughter, shared stories, and the creation of new memories. As they sat together, Clara felt a profound sense of relief and renewed purpose. The bond that had been strained was beginning to heal, and Clara’s heart swelled with hope for the future.

### *Poem: Reconnection*

In the warmth of a mother’s embrace,
We find our way, we find our place.
Through tears and laughter, we mend the past,
A bond renewed, a love that lasts.

## Chapter 6: Healing and Growth

### *Rebuilding Relationships*

In the months that followed their reunion, Clara and her daughters embarked on the delicate journey of rebuilding their relationship. The bond that had been strained by years of separation began to mend through consistent communication. Letters exchanged between them were filled with heartfelt words, bridging the physical distance with emotional closeness. Phone calls and video chats became regular fixtures in their lives, allowing them to share their daily experiences, joys, and challenges.

Clara made frequent visits to see Mia and Sophie, ensuring that they spent holidays and special occasions together. Each visit was a step towards healing, filled with laughter, shared meals, and the simple pleasure of each other's company. The warmth of family gatherings brought back a sense of normalcy and belonging that they had all missed.

Recognizing the importance of addressing her own emotional struggles, Clara sought therapy. The sessions were a journey of self-discovery and healing, allowing her to confront her past and learn to forgive herself. She shared her experiences openly with Mia and Sophie, demonstrating that seeking help and being vulnerable were signs of strength, not weakness. This openness fostered a deeper connection between them, as they saw their mother's courage in confronting her demons.

Clara's poetry evolved alongside her healing process, each verse reflecting her journey of growth and self-acceptance. The therapeutic power of writing became a cornerstone of her recovery, and she often shared her new poems with Mia and Sophie, creating a shared space for their emotions and experiences.

### *A Summer of Connection*

One summer, Clara extended an invitation to Mia and Sophie to spend a few weeks with her in Seabrook. The anticipation of their visit filled Clara with joy and excitement. When the day finally arrived, she welcomed them with open arms, her heart brimming with happiness. The days that followed were a tapestry of cherished moments and new memories.

Together, they explored the charming town of Seabrook, its cobblestone streets and vibrant community events providing the perfect backdrop for their reconnection. They attended local art fairs, music festivals, and farmers' markets, immersing themselves in the town's lively atmosphere. The beach became their favorite retreat, where they spent long afternoons basking in the sun, building sandcastles, and sharing stories as the waves gently lapped at the shore.

Clara introduced Mia and Sophie to the art of poetry, guiding them through the process of expressing their thoughts and feelings through words. They began a family journal, filling its pages with verses, drawings, and reflections. This creative endeavor became a symbol of their healing, a testament to their collective growth and the love that bound them together.

### *An Evening of Reflection*

One evening, as they sat on the porch watching the sunset paint the sky with hues of gold and pink, a profound sense of peace settled over them. The tranquil scene was a stark contrast to the turmoil they had endured, and it felt like a promise of brighter days ahead. Sophie turned to Clara, her eyes reflecting the colors of the setting sun, and said, “Mom, we’re proud of you. You’ve come so far, and we’re so happy to be a part of your life again.”

Clara’s heart swelled with gratitude and love, her emotions spilling over in the form of tears. “I’m proud of you both too,” she replied, her voice trembling with emotion. “You’ve shown me what it means to be strong and resilient. I love you more than words can express.”

As they sat together, enveloped in the warm glow of the sunset, they felt a profound sense of unity and healing. The struggles of the past had forged a stronger bond between them, and they knew that together, they could face whatever the future held.

*Poem: Healing Together*

In the glow of the setting sun,
We find our hearts, we find we're one.
Through the trials, we've come so far,
Together, we heal, a shining star.

## Chapter 7: Discovering the Cottage

### A Family Heirloom

While researching her mother's life at the local library, Clara stumbled upon a mention of an old family property. The reference was in a dusty, forgotten ledger, detailing the history of properties in Seabrook. As Clara read through the entries, she discovered that her mother, Evelyn, had once owned a quaint cottage by the sea. Intrigued and filled with a sense of destiny, Clara decided to visit the cottage, hoping to uncover more about her mother's past.

The cottage, with its ivy-clad façade and quaint charm, stood as a testament to history. Built in the late 1800s, it had originally been a summer retreat for a wealthy family seeking respite from city life. Over the decades, the cottage had witnessed countless seasons and changes, its walls accumulating layers of stories and memories. The exterior was adorned with creeping ivy that lent an air of timelessness, and the well-tended gardens boasted vibrant blooms and ancient trees that whispered secrets of the past.

Inside, the cottage was a treasure trove of antiquities. The air was tinged with the subtle fragrance of aged wood and lavender. Antique furniture, each piece telling its own tale, was scattered throughout the rooms. Shelves were lined with old books whose spines were worn with age, and family heirlooms were displayed with pride. The walls were adorned with portraits and landscapes, each painting capturing a moment from the lives of those who had once called this place home.

Among the cottage's many features was the hidden room, a secret space discovered by Evelyn in her youth. This room, concealed behind a bookshelf, had served as her sanctuary—a place where she could retreat from the world and indulge her passions for writing and painting. It was a haven where her creativity could flourish away from prying eyes.

## The Hidden Room

On a particularly stormy evening, as rain hammered against the windows and wind howled through the trees, Clara and her daughters decided to delve deeper into the cottage's mysteries. The rhythmic patter of raindrops on the roof created a soothing backdrop to their exploration. The cottage, with its crackling fireplace and warm, golden light, felt like a cozy haven against the tempestuous weather outside.

Determined to uncover more about their family's heritage, they decided to spend the evening unraveling the past. The ambiance inside the cottage was one of serene curiosity, contrasting sharply with the chaos of the storm outside. As they rummaged through an old, ornate dresser in the living room, Sophie's fingers brushed against something unusual. With a gasp of excitement, she pulled out an old, intricately designed key from a hidden drawer. The key's delicate engravings and ornate craftsmanship hinted at its age and significance.

Clara's heart skipped a beat as she took the key from Sophie. The intricate patterns on the key seemed to hold a thousand untold stories. “I wonder what this opens,” she mused aloud, her curiosity piqued by the mysterious find.

Mia, always eager for adventure, suggested they search the house for a matching lock. “Let’s start with the living room,” she proposed, her eyes alight with anticipation. “There must be something here.”

They began their search with enthusiasm, inspecting every nook and cranny of the room. The living room, filled with old furniture, ornate rugs, and family heirlooms, was like a labyrinth of history. The scent of aged wood and the soft glow of lamplight added to the sense of stepping back in time. As they moved a stack of dusty books from one of the shelves, Mia noticed a small, nearly imperceptible keyhole nestled behind a bookshelf.

Clara’s breath quickened with excitement as she carefully inserted the key into the keyhole. The bookshelf creaked with age as it swung open, revealing a narrow, winding staircase descending into darkness. The air that wafted up was cool and musty, carrying the faint scent of old wood and forgotten memories.

“Should we go down?” Sophie’s voice was tinged with a mix of eagerness and trepidation.

Clara took a deep breath, her resolve firm. “Let’s see what’s down there,” she said, gripping her daughters’ hands. Together, they descended the stairs, their footsteps echoing softly in the stillness.

At the bottom of the stairs, they discovered the hidden room, a time capsule untouched by the passage of years. The room was a treasure trove of historical artifacts: old photographs, handwritten letters, and keepsakes that narrated the history of Clara’s family. The walls were adorned with paintings of the sea and Seabrook, capturing the town’s changing beauty through the seasons. Each painting seemed to breathe with life, illuminated by a sliver of moonlight streaming through a concealed window.

In one corner of the room, a large, antique desk stood draped in dust but still sturdy, its surface covered with scattered papers and faded ink. Nearby, a trunk overflowed with old toys and garments, relics of a childhood long gone but not forgotten.

As Clara explored the room, she came across a letter addressed to her. With trembling hands, she unfolded it, the creases revealing the handwriting of her mother. The letter was a poignant message of love, regret, and the hope for a future reunion. It was a bridge from the past to the present, linking Clara to the mother she had lost.

The discovery of the hidden room was more than just a journey into the past; it was a profound moment of connection. The artifacts, the letter, and the memories they unearthed helped to bridge the gap between Clara and her daughters, providing a deeper understanding of their shared history and the enduring love that had always bound them together.

**Poem: The Hidden Room**In the shadows of the past, we find,

A mother's love, a heart entwined.

Through letters, art, and memories dear,

We bridge the gap, we draw them near.

## Chapter 8: The Mysterious Neighbor

### *An Unexpected Visitor*

As they continued to explore the hidden room, they heard a soft knock on the door upstairs. Clara and her daughters exchanged puzzled glances before heading back up to the living room. When Clara opened the door, she found an elderly man standing on the porch, his eyes twinkling with a knowing smile.

“Good evening,” he said, tipping his hat. “My name is Mr. Whitaker. I live next door. I couldn’t help but notice the light in the hidden room. I see you’ve found it.”

Clara was taken aback. “You know about the hidden room?” she asked, her curiosity piqued.

Mr. Whitaker nodded. “Oh yes, I’ve known about it for years. Your mother and I were close friends. She told me all about the secrets of this cottage. I thought you might need some help understanding what you’ve found.”

Inviting Mr. Whitaker inside, Clara and her daughters listened intently as he shared stories about their family’s history and the significance of the hidden room. He explained that the room had been a sanctuary for Clara’s mother, a place where she could express her creativity and keep her most cherished memories safe.

### *Mr. Whitaker's Connection to Clara's Mother*

Mr. Whitaker had moved to Seabrook many years ago, shortly after retiring from his career as a history professor. He had always been fascinated by the stories and secrets of old houses, and the cottage next door to his had immediately caught his attention. It wasn't long before he met Clara's mother, Evelyn, who had recently inherited the cottage from her parents.

Evelyn and Mr. Whitaker quickly became friends, bonding over their shared love of history and literature. Evelyn often invited Mr. Whitaker over for tea, and they would spend hours discussing books, poetry, and the history of Seabrook. Mr. Whitaker was captivated by Evelyn's stories about the cottage and its hidden room, a place she had discovered as a young girl.

"Evelyn was an extraordinary woman," Mr. Whitaker said, his voice filled with admiration. "She had a gift for storytelling and a heart full of love. The hidden room was her refuge, a place where she could escape the world and immerse herself in her writing and painting."

Mr. Whitaker knew Evelyn during a particularly challenging time in her life. She had been involved in a tragic car accident while pregnant, and the injuries she sustained meant she wouldn't survive to see her daughter born. Despite the pain and uncertainty, Evelyn remained resilient, pouring her emotions into her art and poetry. Mr. Whitaker often visited her, offering support and companionship during her final months.

"Evelyn confided in me about her past and her fears for the future," Mr. Whitaker continued. "She was deeply worried about what would happen to her unborn daughter, Clara. The hidden room became a place where she could express her love, hope, and regret, capturing her emotions in her art."

Clara felt a lump in her throat as she listened to Mr. Whitaker's words. The hidden room, with its treasures and secrets, became a bridge between the past and the present, helping her understand her mother's love and the legacy she had left behind.

"Evelyn never stopped thinking about you, Clara," Mr. Whitaker said softly. "She always hoped that one day you would find your way back to her. She left clues in the hidden room, hoping you would discover them and understand her love for you."

Clara felt a deep connection to her mother as she absorbed Mr. Whitaker's words. The hidden room, with its artifacts and memories, provided a deeper understanding of their shared history and the enduring love that had always bound them together.

**The Hidden Room's Secrets**

Mr. Whitaker guided Clara and her daughters back to the hidden room, pointing out various items and explaining their significance. He showed them Evelyn's journals, filled with poetry and sketches, and the letters she had written but never sent. Each piece told a story of a woman who had loved deeply and suffered greatly.

"Evelyn was a remarkable artist," Mr. Whitaker said, holding up one of her paintings. "She captured the beauty of Seabrook in her work, but she also painted her dreams and her sorrows. This room is a testament to her resilience and her hope."

As they explored the hidden room together, Clara felt a deep sense of connection to her mother. She realized that the room was not just a place of secrets, but a sanctuary of love and creativity. It was a part of her heritage, a legacy she could share with her daughters.

*A New Understanding*

With Mr. Whitaker's guidance, Clara and her daughters began to piece together the story of their family. They spent hours in the hidden room, reading Evelyn's journals and letters, and discovering the depth of her love and her struggles. The experience brought them closer together, helping them heal and reconnect.

Clara's poetry took on a new dimension, reflecting the joy and pain of finding her mother. Her final collection of poems, titled "Found," became a bestseller, touching the hearts of many who had experienced similar journeys of loss and reunion.

**Poem: Found**

In the shadows of forgotten years,
A whisper of love, a mother's tears.
Hidden in the pages of time's embrace,
A journey of hearts, a sacred space.

Through valleys deep and mountains high,
The echoes of dreams that never die.
In every step, a story unfolds,
Of courage, of hope, of love untold.

Found in the light of a new dawn's rise,
A bond unbroken, a love that ties.
In the tapestry of life, so grand,
Together we walk, hand in hand.

## Chapter 9: Uncovering More Secrets

Certainly! Here is the revised version:

### Discovering More About Evelyn

As Clara delved deeper into the hidden room, she felt a whirlwind of emotions. Each discovery was like a piece of a puzzle, slowly revealing the picture of a woman she had never truly known but had always longed to understand.

The first time Clara found one of Evelyn's journals, she hesitated. The leather-bound book felt heavy in her hands, not just in weight but in the significance it held. As she opened it, the scent of aged paper and ink filled the air, and she could almost feel her mother's presence beside her.

Reading Evelyn's words, Clara felt a mixture of sorrow and connection. The entries were filled with reflections on life, love, and the pain of separation. Evelyn wrote about the tragic car accident she had been involved in while pregnant. The injuries she sustained meant she wouldn't survive to see her daughter born. Tears welled up in Clara's eyes as she read about her mother's anguish and the hope that one day they would be reunited through the legacy she left behind.

Among the journals, Clara found sketches and paintings, each one a testament to Evelyn's talent and her emotional depth. One painting, in particular, caught Clara's eye. It was a portrait of a young girl, her eyes filled with innocence and curiosity. Clara realized it was a self-portrait of Evelyn as a child, and she felt a pang of longing for the mother-daughter bond they had missed out on.

As days turned into weeks, Clara spent countless hours in the hidden room, uncovering more of Evelyn's secrets. She found letters addressed to her, never sent but filled with words of love and regret. Each letter was a window into Evelyn's heart, and Clara cherished them as if they were precious gems.

**Letter 1:**

*My Dearest Clara,*

*If you are reading this, it means you have found your way back to the place where my heart has always been. The accident took so much from me, but the thought of you gave me strength in my final days.*

*I dreamed of the life you would lead, the person you would become. I hoped that you would find love, happiness, and fulfillment. I wanted to be there for you, to guide you, but fate had other plans. Please know that every moment of my life, I carried you in my heart.*

*I left these letters and my art as a way for you to know me, to understand the love I have for you. I hope they bring you comfort and a sense of connection to the mother who loved you more than words can express.*

*With all my love, Evelyn*

Clara didn't keep these discoveries to herself. She shared them with her twin daughters, Sophia and Mia. The girls were captivated by their grandmother's story, and they often joined Clara in the hidden room, listening intently as she read aloud from Evelyn's journals and letters. The hidden room became a place of bonding for the three of them, a sanctuary where they could connect with their family's past and each other.

### *The Intriguing Wooden Box*

One day, while exploring a dusty corner of the hidden room, Sophia stumbled upon a small, intricately carved wooden box. The box was locked, and the key was nowhere to be found. Clara and her daughters were intrigued. What secrets could this box hold? They searched the room meticulously, hoping to find the key that would unlock yet another piece of Evelyn's past.

Meanwhile, Mr. Whitaker watched Clara and her daughters with a mixture of pride and nostalgia. He remembered the day Evelyn had shown him the hidden room for the first time. She had been so full of life and passion, her eyes sparkling as she shared her stories and dreams. Mr. Whitaker had been captivated by her spirit and had cherished their friendship deeply.

When Evelyn passed away, Mr. Whitaker had promised himself that he would keep an eye on the cottage and its secrets, hoping that one day

Clara would return. Seeing Clara now, so determined to uncover her mother's past, filled him with a sense of fulfillment. He knew that Evelyn's legacy was in good hands.

One evening, as Clara and her daughters were about to leave the hidden room, Mr. Whitaker approached them. "I see you've found the box," he said with a gentle smile. "Evelyn mentioned it to me once. She said it held something very precious, something she hoped you would find one day."

Clara looked at Mr. Whitaker, her curiosity piqued. "Do you know where the key might be?" she asked.

Mr. Whitaker nodded slowly. "I believe I do. Evelyn entrusted it to me, with the hope that I would give it to you when the time was right." He reached into his pocket and pulled out a small, ornate key. "I think it's time you discovered what's inside."

With trembling hands, Clara took the key and unlocked the box. Inside, she found a collection of letters, photographs, and a delicate locket. The letters were written by Evelyn, detailing her hopes and dreams for Clara, and the photographs captured moments of Evelyn's life that Clara had never seen. The locket contained a tiny portrait of Evelyn and a lock of her hair.

The locket held a special significance. It was a family heirloom, passed down through generations of women in Evelyn's family. Evelyn had worn it every day, finding comfort in its presence. The tiny portrait inside was of Evelyn herself, painted when she was a young woman, full of dreams and aspirations. The lock of hair was a symbol of the bond between mother and daughter, a tangible piece of Evelyn that Clara could hold close to her heart.

**Letter 2:**

My Beloved Clara,

This locket has been in our family for generations. It was given to me by my mother, and now I pass it on to you. Inside, you will find a portrait of me and a lock of my hair. I hope it brings you comfort and reminds you that I am always with you, no matter where life takes you.

I want you to know that you were my greatest joy, even though we never met. I poured all my love into my art and these letters, hoping that one day you would find them and feel the connection we share. You are a part of me, and I am a part of you.

Wear this locket with pride, my dear Clara. It is a symbol of our unbreakable bond, a bond that transcends time and space. I love you more than words can say, and I will always be with you in spirit.

Forever yours,
Evelyn

As Clara and her daughters pored over the contents of the box, they felt a profound connection to Evelyn. The hidden room, the box, and its treasures became a bridge between the past and the present, helping them understand the depth of Evelyn's love and the legacy she had left behind.

## Chapter 10: The Journey to Star's Haven

### *The Search for Star*

But the box held more than just letters and photographs. Beneath a false bottom, Clara discovered a small, velvet pouch. Inside the pouch was a delicate silver bracelet, adorned with tiny charms. Each charm represented a significant moment in Evelyn's life—a miniature book for her love of literature, a paintbrush for her art, and a heart for her love for Clara.

There was also a small, folded map, marked with a series of cryptic symbols and notes. Clara's curiosity was piqued. What could this map lead to? Was there another hidden treasure, another secret waiting to be uncovered?

As Clara studied the map, she noticed a name written in the corner: "Star." Who was Star, and what connection did she have to Evelyn? Clara's mind raced with possibilities. Could Star be a friend, a confidante, or perhaps a relative she had never known about?

Determined to find out more, Clara and her daughters continued their search. Behind a loose brick in the hidden room, they discovered a small, leather-bound diary. The cover was embossed with the name "Star," and inside, the pages were filled with Evelyn's handwriting.

**Diary Entry 1:**

Dear Star,

From the moment we met, I knew you were someone special. Your spirit, your kindness, and your unwavering support have been a beacon of light in my life. I cherish our friendship more than words can express.

Today, I found out that I am expecting a child. It is both a joyous and terrifying revelation. I wanted you to be the first to know because you have always been my confidante, my rock. I hope you will be there for me as I navigate this new chapter in my life.

With love,
Evelyn

**Diary Entry 2:**

Dear Star,

The accident has changed everything. I am filled with sorrow and fear for the future. The doctors say I won't survive to see my child born. My heart aches with the thought of leaving her alone in this world.

I have decided to leave her clues, pieces of my heart, so that one day she might find them and know how much I loved her. You have always been my guiding star, and I hope you will continue to watch over her in my absence.

With all my love,
Evelyn

As Clara read the diary entries, she felt a deep sense of connection to Star, the mysterious figure who had been such an important part of Evelyn's life. Who was Star, and what role had she played in Evelyn's story? Clara knew that finding out more about Star would be the key to uncovering the full story of her mother's life and the secrets she had kept hidden.

### *The Lighthouse by the Sea*

Clara's journey was one of healing and understanding. She realized that while they had been separated in life, their souls were intertwined through the stories, art, and emotions Evelyn had poured into the hidden room. It was a bridge that connected their hearts across time and space, allowing Clara and her daughters to finally embrace the love Evelyn had always held for them.

As Clara read the diary entries, she felt a growing sense of urgency to visit the lighthouse mentioned by her mother. She shared her thoughts with Mr. Whitaker, who nodded thoughtfully.

"The lighthouse has always been a special place for Evelyn," Mr. Whitaker said. "I remember her telling me about the times she spent there, finding peace and inspiration. If she left something there for you, it must be important."

Clara, Sophia, and Mia decided to visit the lighthouse the next day. The journey was filled with anticipation and a sense of adventure. As they approached the lighthouse, Clara felt a mix of excitement and trepidation. What would they find there?

Inside the lighthouse, they searched every nook and cranny, guided by the clues in Evelyn's diary. Finally, behind a loose stone in the wall, they found a small, weathered box. With trembling hands, Clara opened it.

Inside the box were more letters, photographs, and a small, intricately carved wooden star. The letters were filled with Evelyn's hopes and dreams for Clara, as well as stories about her friendship with Star. The photographs captured moments of Evelyn's life that Clara had never seen, including pictures of Evelyn and Star together, their smiles radiating warmth and happiness.

**Letter 3:**

My Dearest Clara,

If you are reading this, it means you have found the lighthouse and the treasures I left for you. This place has always been a sanctuary for me, a place where I could find peace and inspiration. I hope it will become a special place for you as well.

The wooden star you found is a symbol of my friendship with Star. She has been my guiding light, my confidante, and my rock. I hope you will find comfort in knowing that you have a family who loves you, both in this world and beyond.

With all my love,
Evelyn

As Clara and her daughters pored over the contents of the box, they felt a profound connection to Evelyn and Star. The hidden room, the lighthouse, and the treasures they found became a bridge between the past and the present, helping them understand the depth of Evelyn's love and the legacy she had left behind.

### *The Hidden Documents*

But as they continued to explore the lighthouse, Clara found another hidden compartment. Inside was a bundle of letters tied with a red ribbon. These letters were different, written in a hurried, almost frantic hand. They hinted at a scandal, a secret that Evelyn had been desperate to keep hidden.

**Letter 4:**

Dear Star,

I don't know how much longer I can keep this secret. The truth is tearing me apart. I trusted him, and he betrayed me in the worst possible way. I fear for Clara's future if this ever comes to light. I need your help, Star. You are the only one I can trust.

With all my love,
Evelyn

**Letter 5:**

Dear Star,

He came to the cottage again today, demanding to talk. I refused, but I am terrified of what he might do. I can't let him ruin Clara's life the way he ruined mine. Please, Star, I need your strength and guidance now more than ever.

With all my love,
Evelyn

As Clara read these letters, a chill ran down her spine. Who was this man Evelyn wrote about, and what had he done to her? The letters hinted at a dark secret, a scandal that had haunted Evelyn until her final days. Clara knew she had to uncover the truth, not just for herself, but for her daughters as well.

*The Trip to Star's Haven*

Clara turned her attention back to the map. The cryptic symbols and notes seemed to point to various locations around Seabrook. One note in particular caught her eye: "Star's Haven." Could this be a place where Star lived or a location significant to her?

Determined to find out more, Clara decided to follow the map's clues. She shared her plan with Mr. Whitaker, who offered to help. "I remember hearing about a place called Star's Haven," he said. "It's an old cottage on the outskirts of town. It was said to be a retreat for artists and writers, a place of inspiration and solitude."

With renewed determination, Clara, Sophia, Mia, and Mr. Whitaker set out to find Star's Haven. The journey took them through winding roads and dense forests, each step filled with anticipation. When they finally arrived, they found an enchanting cottage nestled among the trees, its walls covered in ivy and its windows glowing with a warm, inviting light.

As they stepped inside, the history of Star's Haven began to unfold before them. The cottage had been built in the late 1800s by a reclusive artist named Elara Starling, known simply as Star. She was a visionary, ahead of her time, and her works were filled with ethereal beauty and profound emotion. Star's Haven became a sanctuary for her and a select group of artists and writers who sought refuge from the chaos of the outside world.

Elara Starling was not just an artist but also a mystic. She believed that creativity was a divine gift, and she dedicated her life to exploring the spiritual dimensions of art. Her journals, found in a hidden drawer of an antique desk, revealed her deep connection to the natural world and her belief in the power of the unseen. She wrote of visions and dreams that guided her work, and her paintings often depicted otherworldly landscapes and celestial beings.

The cottage itself was designed to be a place of inspiration. Each room was filled with light and adorned with intricate carvings and murals. The garden, now overgrown, had once been a masterpiece of botanical art, with rare flowers and plants arranged in symbolic patterns. Elara Starling's influence attracted many talented individuals, and Star's Haven became a hub of creativity and collaboration.

*The Secret Journal*

Among the items, they found a journal that seemed to hold the key to the scandal Evelyn had hinted at.

**Journal Entry 1:**

Dear Evelyn,

I have always admired your strength and resilience. The way you have faced life's challenges with grace and courage is truly inspiring. I want you to know that I am here for you, no matter what. Together, we can overcome anything.

With love,
Star

**Journal Entry 2:**

Dear Evelyn,

I am deeply troubled by what you have told me. This man, this betrayer, must be held accountable for his actions. We cannot let him continue to harm you or Clara. I will do everything in my power to protect you both.

With love,
Star

**Journal Entry 3:**

Dear Evelyn,

I have discovered something that may help us. There are records and documents that prove his involvement in the scandal. He has been using his position to manipulate and control others, and I believe we can expose him. I have hidden these documents in a safe place, and I will share their location with you when the time is right.

With love,
Star

As Clara read Star's journal entry, she felt a surge of determination. The documents Star mentioned could be the key to uncovering the truth about the man who had tormented Evelyn. Clara knew she had to find these documents to understand the full extent of the scandal and to protect her family.

Clara, Sophia, Mia, and Mr. Whitaker continued to search Star's Haven, looking for any clues that might lead them to the hidden documents. In a small, locked drawer, they found a key and a note from Star.

**Note:**

Evelyn,

The key you found will unlock the chest in the attic. Inside, you will find the documents that reveal the truth. Use them wisely and protect Clara at all costs.

With love,
Star

With the key in hand, Clara and her daughters made their way to the attic. The chest was old and covered in dust, but the key fit perfectly. Inside, they found a stack of documents, letters, and photographs. As they sifted through the contents, the full extent of the scandal began to unfold.

The documents revealed that the man Evelyn had written about was a powerful figure in the community, someone who had used his influence to manipulate and control others. He had betrayed Evelyn's trust in a deeply personal way, and she had been determined to protect Clara from his reach.

Among the documents, they found a letter from Evelyn to Star, detailing her fears and the steps she had taken to safeguard Clara's future.

**Letter 6:**

Dear Star,

I have done everything I can to protect Clara from him. The documents you found are crucial to exposing his actions, but I fear the consequences. If anything happens to me, please ensure that Clara is safe and that the truth comes to light.

With all my love,
Evelyn

As Clara read the letter, she felt a mix of anger and sadness. The man who had caused her mother so much pain had to be held accountable. She knew that uncovering the truth was the only way to honor Evelyn's memory and protect her family.

## Chapter 11: Exposing the Truth

### *The Plan*

With the documents in hand, Clara and her daughters returned to Seabrook. They shared their findings with Mr. Whitaker, who offered his support and guidance. Together, they began to piece together the evidence and prepare to expose the man who had tormented Evelyn.

Clara's journey was far from over. There were still mysteries to unravel, secrets to uncover, and a legacy of love and pain to explore. But with the support of her family and friends, she felt ready to face whatever challenges lay ahead.

As they worked to uncover the truth, Clara felt a deep sense of connection to her mother and to Star. The hidden room, the lighthouse, and Star's Haven had become bridges between the past and the present, helping her understand the depth of Evelyn's love and the legacy she had left behind.

The locket, now worn by Clara, became a symbol of this enduring connection. It was a reminder of the love that transcended time and space, a love that would continue to guide and inspire Clara and her daughters for generations to come.

And as they prepared to expose the scandal and seek justice, Clara knew that Evelyn's spirit was with them, guiding them every step of the way.

*Discovering the Truth About Her Father*

As they sifted through more documents, Clara found a photograph. It was a picture of a man standing next to a young woman who looked strikingly familiar, they were holding hands. Clara's heart skipped a beat as she realized the woman was Evelyn, her mother. "Could this man be... my father?" Clara whispered, her voice trembling with a mix of fear and hope.

The possibility that the man in the photograph was her father, a prominent and wealthy married man, added a new layer of mystery. Clara had grown up in an orphanage, knowing nothing about her parents. The idea that he could be involved in a scandal and might have even orchestrated the car accident that killed her mother was almost too much to bear.

"We need to find out more about him," Clara said, her resolve hardening. "If he is my father, and if he had anything to do with my mom's death, we need to bring him to justice."

Her daughters nodded in agreement, their faces set with determination. Clara's resolve hardened as she stared at the photograph. "If he is my father, and if he had anything to do with the accident, we need to uncover the truth," she said, her voice steady despite the turmoil inside her.

Mr. Whitaker nodded, his expression serious. “We’ll need to dig deeper into his background and find any connections he might have had with Evelyn. This could be dangerous, Clara. Are you sure you’re ready for this?”

Clara took a deep breath, feeling the weight of the locket around her neck. “I have to be. For my mother, for my daughters, and for myself. We deserve to know the truth.”

## Chapter 12: Uncovering the Final Truths

### *Investigating the Past*

Clara, with the help of Mr. Whitaker and her daughters, delved into the investigation. They started with the documents from Star’s Haven, which included financial records, letters, and even some newspaper clippings about the wealthy and influential man who seemed to have had a connection with Evelyn. They found his name: Richard Kensington.

Richard was a respected businessman in Seabrook, known for his charitable contributions and social standing. However, the documents revealed a darker side: affairs, manipulations, and possible involvement in illegal activities. Clara felt a cold shiver as she realized the extent of his deceit.

Clara reached out to old friends and acquaintances who might remember Richard and Evelyn’s relationship. She found a few who hinted at the scandal, confirming that Richard had indeed been involved with Evelyn but had denied it publicly, fearing it would ruin his reputation and marriage.

### *Confronting the Past*

With enough evidence in hand, Clara decided it was time to confront Richard. She wrote a letter, requesting a meeting under the pretense of discussing charitable work. Richard agreed, unaware of Clara’s true intentions.

The meeting took place at a local café, the same one where Clara had worked and found solace years ago. As Richard arrived, Clara’s heart pounded. She recognized the man from the photograph immediately, his face aged but still imposing.

“Mr. Kensington,” Clara began, her voice steady but filled with underlying emotion, “Thank you for meeting with me.”

Richard smiled politely. “Of course. What can I help you with?”

Clara took a deep breath. “I’m here to talk about Evelyn. Evelyn Montgomery.”

Richard’s smile faltered. “I’m not sure I understand.”

“I think you do,” Clara said, pulling out the photograph of Richard and Evelyn. “This is you, isn’t it? And Evelyn... she’s my mother.”

Richard’s face turned pale. “How... how did you find this?”

“It doesn’t matter how I found it. What matters is that you answer for what you did. I have documents, letters, and testimonies that connect you to a scandal involving my mother. And I believe you were involved in her accident.”

Richard’s eyes widened in panic. “You have no idea what you’re talking about.”

Clara’s resolve hardened. “I know enough. And I will not rest until the truth is out. You may have escaped justice back then, but not anymore.”

*Seeking Justice*

With Richard's reaction confirming her suspicions, Clara knew she had to act quickly. She and Mr. Whitaker compiled all the evidence and presented it to the authorities. An investigation was launched, and the truth about Richard Kensington's actions began to unravel.

News of the scandal spread quickly through Seabrook. The once-respected businessman was now facing charges of fraud, manipulation, and potential involvement in Evelyn's death. Clara's story, as well as her mother's, was finally getting the attention and justice it deserved.

## Chapter 13: Finding Peace and Moving Forward

*Rebuilding Relationships*

With Richard's downfall, Clara felt a weight lift from her shoulders. She had honored her mother's memory by uncovering the truth and ensuring justice. Now, she focused on rebuilding her life and her relationship with her daughters.

Mia and Sophie, inspired by their mother's courage, began to reconnect with her on a deeper level. They spent more time together, exploring Seabrook, writing poetry, and sharing their thoughts and dreams. Clara's bond with her daughters grew stronger, filled with understanding and love.

### *Embracing the Legacy*

Clara's journey of uncovering her past and seeking justice for her mother led her to appreciate the strength and resilience she had inherited from Evelyn. She decided to compile her mother's writings and paintings into a book, preserving Evelyn's legacy and sharing her story with the world.

The book, titled "Echoes of Love," became a bestseller, touching the hearts of many who read it. Clara's poetry, combined with Evelyn's art and letters, created a powerful testament to the enduring power of love and resilience.

### *A New Beginning*

Clara, Mia, and Sophie stood on the shore of Seabrook's beach, watching the sunset. The sky was painted with hues of orange and pink, a beautiful backdrop for a moment of reflection and peace.

"Mom, you've been amazing through all of this," Sophie said, holding Clara's hand. "We're so proud of you."

Clara smiled, tears of joy in her eyes. "I couldn't have done it without you both. Your love and support mean everything to me."

Mia nodded, wrapping her arm around Clara. "We're a family, and we'll always be there for each other."

As the sun dipped below the horizon, Clara felt a profound sense of closure. The journey had been long and painful, but it had also brought healing and understanding. She looked at her daughters, their faces illuminated by the soft glow of the setting sun, and felt a deep gratitude for the love that had carried them through.

"In the end, love is what sustains us," Clara whispered, more to herself than anyone else. "It's what keeps us connected, no matter the distance or time."

The three of them stood there, embracing the warmth of the moment, knowing that they had found their way back to each other. The future was still uncertain, but they faced it together, with hearts full of love and hope.

## Chapter 14: Revisiting Star Haven

### *A Journey Back*

One sunny afternoon, Clara and her daughters decided to revisit Star Haven. The lighthouse stood tall and proud, a beacon of hope and mystery. As they approached, Clara felt a familiar sense of connection, as if Evelyn's spirit was guiding them once more.

Inside the hidden room, they found more documents and artifacts that hinted at Star's life. Star, it seemed, was not just a guardian of the lighthouse but also a woman with a rich and complex history. Her journals, filled with vivid descriptions and heartfelt entries, painted a picture of a woman who had faced many challenges and had a deep connection to the sea.

### *Discovering Star's Legacy*

As they read through the journals, Clara discovered that Star had been a healer and a protector of the coastal community. She had used her knowledge of herbs and natural remedies to help those in need. Her compassion and strength had earned her the respect and admiration of the townspeople.

One entry, in particular, caught Clara's attention. It spoke of a hidden treasure, a legacy that Star had safeguarded for future generations. The entry was cryptic, mentioning a map and a series of clues that would lead to the treasure's location.

Intrigued, Clara, Sophie, and Mia decided to follow the clues. The first clue led them to the base of the lighthouse, where they found an old, weathered map hidden in a crevice. The map depicted the coastline and marked several key locations with symbols that corresponded to Star's journal entries.

Their adventure took them to various landmarks around Seabrook, each location revealing more about Star's life and the treasure she had hidden. Along the way, they encountered townspeople who shared stories about Star, adding depth to their understanding of her legacy.

### *Uncovering the Treasure*

As they pieced together the clues, Clara felt a growing sense of connection to Star. It was as if Star's spirit was guiding them, just as Evelyn's had. The journey was not just about finding the treasure but also about understanding the legacy of love, resilience, and protection that Star had left behind.

Finally, the clues led them to a secluded cove, where they found a hidden cave. Inside the cave, they discovered a chest filled with Star's treasures—old coins, jewelry, and artifacts that told the story of her life and her connection to the sea.

Among the treasures, Clara found two identical bracelets, intricately designed with symbols of the sea and stars. She held them up, feeling a sense of awe and reverence. "These must be for you," she said, turning to Sophie and Mia. "Star left these for you."

Sophie and Mia's eyes widened with wonder as they took the bracelets. The bracelets seemed to glow with a soft, ethereal light, as if imbued with Star's spirit. Each daughter slipped a bracelet onto her wrist, feeling an immediate connection to the legacy of Star Haven.

"These bracelets are beautiful," Mia whispered, her voice filled with emotion. "It's like Star knew we would find them."

Clara nodded, her heart swelling with pride and love for her daughters. "Star's legacy is now part of you. These bracelets are a symbol of the strength, love, and resilience that she embodied. Wear them as a reminder of the journey we've taken and the bond we share."

As they stood in the cave, Clara felt a sense of peace and fulfillment. The adventure had not only uncovered the secrets of Star Haven but also strengthened the bond between her and her daughters. The lighthouse, Star's Haven, and the treasures they had found became symbols of their enduring connection to the past and their commitment to the future.

With the twin bracelets on their wrists, Sophie and Mia felt a renewed sense of purpose. They knew that their journey was far from over, but they were ready to face whatever challenges lay ahead, guided by the spirits of Evelyn and Star.

## Epilogue: The Legacy of Star Haven

### *An Enduring Connection*

Years passed, and the story of Clara, Sophie, and Mia became a cherished part of Seabrook's history. The lighthouse, Star's Haven, stood as a beacon of hope and resilience, its light guiding sailors and townspeople alike. The legacy of Evelyn and Star continued to inspire and protect the coastal community.

Clara, now a grandmother, often shared the tale of their adventures with her grandchildren. Sophie and Mia, each wearing their twin bracelets, had grown into strong, compassionate women, carrying forward the values and lessons they had learned from their mother and the women who came before them.

### *Honoring the Past*

Sophie became a historian, dedicating her life to preserving the stories and heritage of Seabrook. She wrote a book about their journey, detailing the secrets they uncovered and the strength they found in their family's legacy. Her work brought the community closer together, reminding everyone of the importance of remembering and honoring the past.

Mia, with her intuitive nature, became a healer, much like Star. She used her knowledge of herbs and natural remedies to help those in need, earning the respect and admiration of the townspeople. Her practice grew, and she often felt Star's spirit guiding her, just as it had guided Clara.

### *A Family Celebration*

One summer evening, the family gathered at Star's Haven for a special celebration. The lighthouse was adorned with lights, and the air was filled with the scent of the sea. Clara stood at the base of the lighthouse, looking out at the horizon, her heart full of gratitude and love.

As the sun set, casting a golden glow over the water, Clara's grandchildren ran around, their laughter echoing through the air. Sophie and Mia joined Clara, each holding the hand of one of their children. The twin bracelets on their wrists shimmered in the fading light, a symbol of the enduring connection between the past and the present.

Clara turned to her daughters, her eyes filled with pride. "We've come a long way, haven't we? From uncovering the secrets of our family to building a future filled with love and hope."

Sophie nodded, her eyes shining. "And it's all because of the strength and resilience passed down to us. Evelyn and Star's legacy lives on in us and in our children."

Mia smiled, her voice soft. "We've created a new chapter in our family's story, one that honors the past and looks forward to the future. Star's Haven will always be a place of love, healing, and connection."

As the first stars appeared in the night sky, Clara felt a deep sense of peace. The journey had been long and filled with challenges, but it had also brought them closer together and revealed the true strength of their family's legacy. The lighthouse, Star's Haven, and the twin bracelets were symbols of their enduring bond, guiding them through the generations.

And so, the legacy of Star Haven continued, a testament to the love, resilience, and spirit of the women who had come before and the generations yet to come. The light of the lighthouse shone brightly, a beacon of hope and inspiration for all who followed.

**Whispers of Star Haven**

In the glow of the lighthouse, where the sea meets the sky,
Lies a haven of secrets, where spirits never die.
Star's light guides the weary, through the darkest of nights,
A beacon of hope, in its steadfast, gentle light.

Twin bracelets of beauty, with charms of the sea,
Hold stories of courage, and love's legacy.

From Evelyn's whispers, to Clara's brave quest,
The bonds of their journey, forever will rest.

In the heart of Star Haven, where the past and present blend,
Lies a tale of resilience, that time cannot end.
For generations to come, under the stars' gentle gleam,
The legacy of love, will continue to dream.

## Echoes of Love: A Collection of Poems by Clara

### *Whispers of the Sea*

Beneath the waves, the secrets lie,
Whispers of the sea, a lullaby.
In every crest, a tale is told,
Of love, of loss, of hearts grown bold.

### *A Mother's Lament*

In the mirror, I see her face,
A mother lost, a fall from grace.
Her children cry, she cannot hear,
Her heart is filled with doubt and fear.

*The Hidden Room*

In shadows deep, where secrets sleep,
A hidden room, where hearts do weep.
Letters, art, and memories dear,
A mother's love, forever near.

*The Distance Grows*

In the quiet of the night, I hear their cries,
A mother's love, a fragile guise.
I reach out, but they slip away,
In my heart, they forever stay.

*A Mother's Sacrifice*

In the quiet of the night, I hear their laughter,
A distant echo, a haunting after.
Their faces in my dreams, so near,
Yet in the waking world, they disappear.

*A Beacon of Hope*

Beneath the weight of night, my heart does break,
A sea of tears, an endless ache.
Yet in the dark, a light persists,
A beacon of hope, in the fog and mist.

*Reconnection*

In the warmth of a mother's embrace,
We find our way, we find our place.
Through tears and laughter, we mend the past,
A bond renewed, a love that lasts.

*Healing Together*

In the glow of the setting sun,
We find our hearts, we find we're one.
Through the trials, we've come so far,
Together, we heal, a shining star.

*Found*

In the shadows of forgotten years,
A whisper of love, a mother's tears.
Hidden in the pages of time's embrace,
A journey of hearts, a sacred space.

*Whispers of Star Haven*

In the glow of the lighthouse, where the sea meets the sky,
Lies a haven of secrets, where spirits never die.
Star's light guides the weary, through the darkest of nights,
A beacon of hope, in its steadfast, gentle light.

*Legacy of Love*

Twin bracelets of beauty, with charms of the sea,
Hold stories of courage, and love's legacy.
From Evelyn's whispers, to Clara's brave quest,
The bonds of their journey, forever will rest.

*Timeless Bond*

In the heart of Star Haven, where the past and present blend,
Lies a tale of resilience, that time cannot end.
For generations to come, under the stars' gentle gleam,
The legacy of love, will continue to dream.

## Character Backstories

**Mr. Whitaker's Backstory**: Mr. Whitaker had moved to Seabrook many years ago, shortly after retiring from his career as a history professor. He had always been fascinated by the stories and secrets of old houses, and the cottage next door to his had immediately caught his attention. It wasn't long before he met Clara's mother, Evelyn, who had recently inherited the cottage from her own parents. Evelyn and Mr. Whitaker quickly became friends, bonding over their shared love of history and literature. Evelyn often invited Mr. Whitaker over for tea, and they would spend hours discussing books, poetry, and the history of Seabrook. Mr. Whitaker was captivated by Evelyn's stories about the cottage and its hidden room, a place she had discovered as a young girl.

When Evelyn passed away, Mr. Whitaker had promised himself that he would keep an eye on the cottage and its secrets, hoping that one day Clara would return. Seeing Clara now, so determined to uncover her mother's past, filled him with a sense of fulfillment. He knew that Evelyn's legacy was in good hands.

**Margaret's Backstory**: Margaret, the kind-hearted owner of the café where Clara worked, had an artistic past of her own. She had once been a renowned painter, her works celebrated in galleries across the country. However, a tragic fire had destroyed her studio and most of her life's work, leaving her devastated. Seeking solace, Margaret moved to Seabrook, where she opened the café and found a new purpose in life. The café became her sanctuary, a place where she could surround herself with the warmth of people and the scent of freshly brewed coffee. When Clara came into her life, Margaret saw a reflection of her younger self in the struggling artist and decided to help her in any way she could. Her support and friendship became a cornerstone of Clara's new life in Seabrook.

**Evelyn's Backstory**: Evelyn Montgomery had been a vibrant and talented artist with a deep connection to the sea. Growing up in Seabrook, she spent her childhood exploring the town's hidden nooks and crannies, often sketching the scenes that captivated her imagination. Her parents had owned the cottage near the lighthouse, and it was there that Evelyn discovered the hidden room, which became her sanctuary. After her parents passed away, Evelyn inherited the cottage and continued to pour her heart into her art. She met Clara's father during one of her exhibitions, and their brief but passionate relationship resulted in Clara's birth. Tragically, Evelyn was involved in a car accident while pregnant, leading to complications that ultimately claimed her life shortly after Clara was born. Evelyn's love for her daughter was evident in the letters and artwork she left behind, creating a legacy that Clara would later uncover.

### Historical Context

**Seabrook's Historical Context**: Seabrook was a town steeped in history, its origins dating back to the late 1700s when it was established as a small fishing village. The town's founders, a group of intrepid settlers, were drawn to the area by the rich fishing grounds and the promise of a new life. Over the centuries, Seabrook grew into a bustling port, with ships from all over the world docking at its harbors. The lighthouse, built in the early 1800s, became a crucial navigational aid, guiding sailors safely to shore and earning its place as the town’s most iconic landmark.

**Star Haven and Its Significance**: Star Haven, the enchanting cottage near the lighthouse, had its own unique history. Built in the late 1800s by Elara Starling, a reclusive artist known as Star, the cottage was designed to be a sanctuary for creativity and inspiration. Star was a visionary who believed in the spiritual dimensions of art, and she dedicated her life to exploring the connections between nature, creativity, and the human spirit. Her influence attracted many talented individuals, and Star Haven became a hub for artists and writers seeking refuge from the chaos of the outside world.

**Local Legends and Historical Events**: Seabrook was rich with local legends and historical events that added to its charm. One of the most enduring tales was that of the "Ghost Ship of Seabrook," a shipwreck that occurred in the early 1900s. According to legend, the ship appeared out of the mist one stormy night, its crew lost to the sea. The lighthouse keeper at the time, a man named Jonathan Whitaker (an ancestor of Mr. Whitaker), had witnessed the event and dedicated his life to ensuring such a tragedy would never happen again. His dedication and the subsequent improvements to the lighthouse's design and operation were credited with saving countless lives over the years.

Another notable event was the Great Seabrook Fire of 1924, which nearly destroyed the town. The fire had started in a warehouse and quickly spread through the wooden buildings, fueled by strong winds. The townspeople, led by the local fire brigade, fought valiantly to save their homes and businesses. The aftermath of the fire saw a period of rebuilding, with many of the town's historic buildings being restored or rebuilt using more fire-resistant materials. This event marked a turning point in Seabrook's history, leading to a renewed sense of community and resilience.

These additions provide a richer context for the story, adding depth to the characters and the setting without altering the main content.

## Map of Seabrook and Surrounding Areas

**Title: Map of Seabrook and Star Haven**

**Map Elements:**

**Seabrook Town Center:**

- A bustling area with cobblestone streets.
- Key locations: The local café where Clara worked, the bookstore where she lived, and the historic library.

**Seabrook Lighthouse:**

- Positioned on a rocky promontory.
- An iconic landmark guiding sailors to safety.
- Adjacent to Star Haven, hidden behind ivy-clad walls.

**Star Haven Cottage:**

- Nestled near the lighthouse.
- Surrounded by dense forest and picturesque gardens.

- Marked with significant landmarks such as the hidden room and the attic with the chest.

**Seabrook Beach:**

- A serene coastline where Clara and her daughters often walked.
- Symbolic for its connection to Clara's past and present.

**The Cove:**

- A secluded spot marked by cliffs and crashing waves.
- Location of the hidden cave with Star's treasures.

**Mr. Whitaker's Home:**

- Located next to the cottage.
- A charming home with historical artifacts and a well-tended garden.

**Margaret's Café:**

- A cozy establishment with mismatched furniture and a warm atmosphere.
- Central to Clara's new life in Seabrook.

**Sunnyvale:**

- The charming town Clara moved to after leaving the orphanage.
- Known for its cobblestone streets and vibrant arts community.

**Havenbrook Orphanage:**

- Where Clara spent her childhood.
- A large, somber building on the edge of Havenbrook.

**Map Design:**

- **Style:** Vintage, hand-drawn look with sepia tones to evoke a sense of history and nostalgia.
- **Details:** Include small illustrations of key landmarks like the lighthouse, the café, and the hidden cave. Use a legend to mark significant locations.
- **Borders:** Decorate the map borders with artistic representations of waves, books, and lighthouses.

## Appendices

### *Appendix A: Character Backstories*

**Clara Montgomery:** Born on a stormy night in the coastal town of Havenbrook, Clara Montgomery's life was marked by loss from the very beginning. Her mother, Evelyn, a struggling artist, passed away shortly after giving birth. Clara grew up in an orphanage, finding solace in the worn-out notebook filled with her mother's sketches and poems. As an adult, Clara moved to Seabrook, seeking a fresh start and finding work at a local café. Her life took a turn when she fell in love with Daniel, a regular customer, but their relationship ended when she became pregnant and Daniel left. Clara raised her twin daughters, Mia and Sophie, alone, facing numerous challenges but always finding strength in her poetry.

**Mia and Sophie Montgomery:** Mia and Sophie are Clara's twin daughters, each with distinct personalities that complement each other. Mia is the more outgoing and adventurous of the two, often acting as the leader in their childhood escapades. Sophie, on the other hand, is introspective and sensitive, finding comfort in books and creative activities. Growing up with their single mother, they experienced both the warmth of Clara's love and the struggles of their strained relationship. Their bond with their mother was tested but ultimately strengthened through the challenges they faced together.

**Mr. Whitaker:** An elderly neighbor living next door to the cottage Clara inherited, Mr. Whitaker is a retired history professor with a deep connection to Seabrook. He moved to the town years ago, captivated by its rich history and the charm of its coastal landscape. Mr. Whitaker befriended Evelyn, Clara's mother, and became a confidante and protector of her secrets. His knowledge of the town's history and his insights into Evelyn's life make him an invaluable ally to Clara as she uncovers her past.

**Margaret:** Margaret is the kind-hearted owner of the local café where Clara works. With an artistic past of her own, Margaret immediately connects with Clara and becomes a maternal figure to her. She offers Clara not only employment but also a small apartment above the café, providing a safe haven for Clara and her daughters. Margaret's support and wisdom help Clara navigate the challenges of single motherhood and her journey to uncover her family's secrets.

**Evelyn Montgomery:** Evelyn was a talented but struggling artist whose life was cut short shortly after giving birth to Clara. Her deep connection to the sea and her artistic spirit are evident in her sketches and poems, which she left behind in a worn-out notebook. Evelyn's life was marked by a tragic car accident during her pregnancy, leading to a series of decisions that impacted Clara's future. Her hidden room in the cottage and the secrets she left behind play a crucial role in Clara's journey of discovery.

## *Appendix B: Historical Context of Seabrook*

**Seabrook:** Seabrook is a picturesque coastal town with a rich history dating back to the late 1800s. Founded as a fishing village, it grew into a thriving community known for its vibrant arts scene and close-knit residents. The town's cobblestone streets and historic buildings reflect its storied past, with each corner holding tales of love, loss, and resilience.

**The Lighthouse:** An iconic feature of Seabrook, the lighthouse stands tall on a rocky promontory, guiding ships safely to shore for generations. Built in the early 1900s, it has withstood numerous storms and remains a symbol of hope and guidance for the town's residents. The lighthouse plays a significant role in Clara's journey, serving as both a physical and metaphorical beacon.

**Star Haven:** Star Haven, once a retreat for artists and writers, was founded by Elara Starling, a visionary artist and mystic. The cottage, nestled among trees and overlooking the sea, became a sanctuary for those seeking inspiration and solitude. Elara's legacy, filled with tales of creativity and spiritual exploration, is intricately woven into the fabric of Seabrook's history.

## *Appendix C: Legends and Lore of Seabrook*

**Elara Starling:** Elara Starling, known simply as Star, was a reclusive artist whose works captured the ethereal beauty of the sea and sky. Believed to have had mystical abilities, Star used her art to explore the spiritual dimensions of life. Her journals, filled with vivid descriptions of visions and dreams, offer a glimpse into her unique worldview and her deep connection to the natural world.

**The Hidden Room:** The hidden room in the cottage, discovered by Evelyn in her youth, was a place of refuge and creativity. Filled with her art, letters, and poems, it became a sanctuary where she could express her deepest emotions. The room's secrets, passed down to Clara, serve as a bridge between past and present, revealing the enduring legacy of love and resilience.

**Local Legends:** Seabrook is rich with local legends, from tales of shipwrecks and lost treasures to stories of ghostly apparitions seen near the lighthouse. One popular legend speaks of a ship called The Star's Grace, which supposedly vanished in a storm, only to reappear years later with its crew unharmed, guided back by the lighthouse's beam. These legends add a layer of mystique to the town and contribute to its enchanting atmosphere.

Here is the sketch-like illustration of Elara Starling, also known as Star. The mystical and dreamlike style captures her unique connection to the natural world and her spiritual abilities.

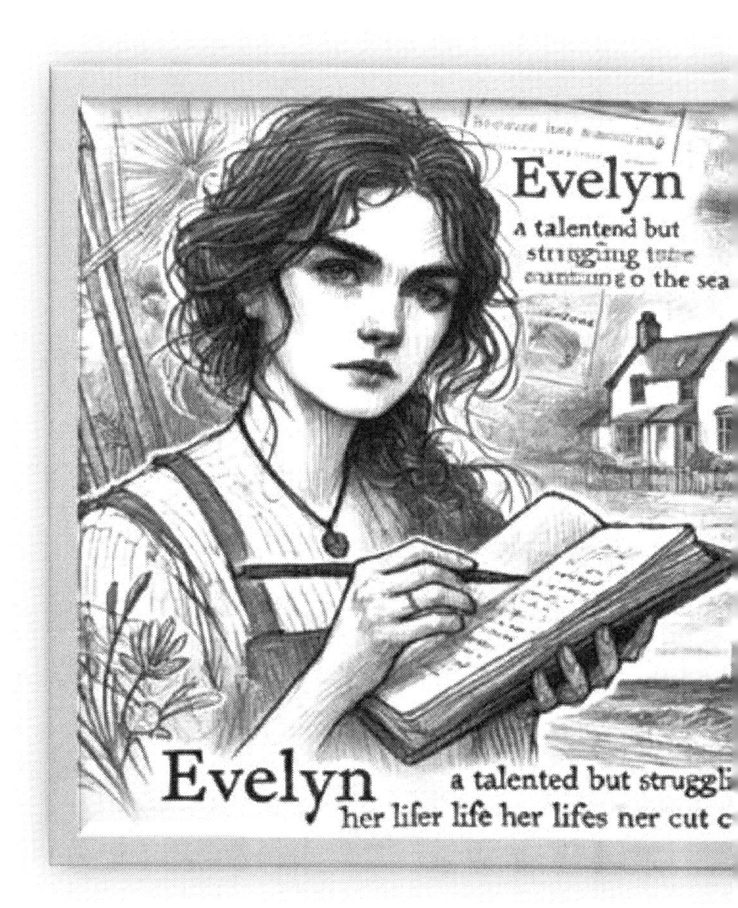


Here is the sketch-like illustration of Evelyn, the talented but struggling artist, holding her worn-out notebook filled with sketches and poems. The background includes elements of the sea and a hint of the hidden room in the cottage.

**A Note to the Grandsons of Harriett Atherton Croskrey**

This book is inspired by the beautiful poetry of Harriett Atherton Croskrey, whose words continue to resonate with love and wisdom. To her beloved grandsons, know that she cherished each of you deeply. Her love for you was boundless, and she often spoke of the joy you brought into her life.

If Memaw were alive today, she would be immensely proud of each of you. Your accomplishments, your kindness, and the way you carry her legacy forward in your hearts and actions would fill her with pride. She believed in you and saw the potential for greatness in each of you.

Her poetry and ancestorial research were her way of sharing her love, hopes, and dreams. As you read this book, remember that her spirit lives on in every word, and her love continues to guide and inspire you. You are her greatest legacy, and she would be overjoyed to see the men you have become.

Made in the USA
Middletown, DE
07 September 2024